Creeds
to
Love
and
Live
By

Other books by

Blue Mountain Press INC.

Come Into the Mountains, Dear Friend
by Susan Polis Schutz
I Want to Laugh, I Want to Cry
by Susan Polis Schutz
Peace Flows from the Sky
by Susan Polis Schutz
Someone Else to Love
by Susan Polis Schutz
I'm Not That Kind of Girl
by Susan Polis Schutz
Yours If You Ask
by Susan Polis Schutz
The Best Is Yet to Be
Step to the Music You Hear, Vol. I
The Language of Friendship
The Language of Love
The Language of Happiness
The Desiderata of Happiness
by Max Ehrmann
Whatever Is, Is Best
by Ella Wheeler Wilcox
Poor Richard's Quotations
by Benjamin Franklin
I Care About Your Happiness
by Kahlil Gibran/Mary Haskell
My Life and Love Are One
by Vincent Van Gogh
I Wish You Good Spaces
by Gordon Lightfoot
We Are All Children Searching for Love
by Leonard Nimoy
Come Be with Me
by Leonard Nimoy
Catch Me with Your Smile
by Peter McWilliams
On the Wings of Friendship
Think of Me Kindly
by Ludwig van Beethoven
You've Got a Friend
Carole King
I Want You to Be Happy
by Hoyt Axton
With You There and Me Here

Creeds
to
Love
and
Live
By

Edited by SandPiper Studios

Designs adapted from the
works of the Roycrofters

Blue Mountain Press ™.

Boulder, Colorado

Copyright © SandPiper Studios, Inc., 1978.
All rights reserved, including the right to
reproduce this book or portions thereof in any form.

Library of Congress Number: 77-93902
ISBN: 0-88396-027-3

Manufactured in the United States of America

First Printing: June, 1978
Second Printing: January, 1979

ACKNOWLEDGMENTS are on page 63.

Blue Mountain Press INC

P.O. Box 4549, Boulder, Colorado 80306

CONTENTS

hat lies
behind us
and what lies
before us
are tiny matters compared to
what lies within us.

— Ralph Waldo Emerson

romise yourself to be so
strong that nothing can
disturb your peace of mind.
To talk health, happiness
and prosperity to every person you meet.
To make all your friends feel that there
is something in them. To look at the
sunny side of everything and make your
optimism come true. To think only of
the best, to work only for the best and
expect only the best. To be just as
enthusiastic about the success of others
as you are about your own. To forget the
mistakes of the past and press on to
the greater achievements of the future.
To wear a cheerful countenance at all times
and give every living creature you meet
a smile. To give so much time to the
improvement of yourself that you have
no time to criticize others. To be too large
for worry, too noble for anger, too
strong for fear and too happy to permit
the presence of trouble.

— Christian D. Larson

GIVE ME

Give me work to do,
Give me health,
Give me joy in
simple things,
Give me an eye for beauty,
A tongue for truth,
A heart that loves,
A mind that reasons,
A sympathy that understands.
Give me neither malice nor envy,
But a true kindness
And a noble common sense.
At the close of each day
Give me a book
And a friend with whom
I can be silent.

— S. M. Frazier

MY CREED

I would be true, for there
are those who trust me;
I would be pure, for there
are those who care;
I would be strong, for there is much to suffer;
I would be brave, for there is much to dare.
I would be friend of all — the foe — the friendless;
I would be giving and forget the gift;
I would be humble, for I know my weakness;
I would look up and laugh — and love — and lift.

— Howard Arnold Walter

RESOLUTION

et then our first act
every morning be to
make the following
resolve for the day:
I shall not fear anyone on earth.
I shall fear only God.
I shall not bear ill will toward anyone.
I shall not submit to injustice from anyone.
I shall conquer untruth by truth.
And in resisting untruth I shall put up with
   all suffering.

— Mahatma Gandhi

 will start anew
this morning
with a higher,
fairer creed;
I will cease to stand complaining
of my ruthless neighbor's greed;
I will cease to sit repining while
my duty's call is clear;
I will waste no moment whining and
my heart shall know no fear.

I will look sometimes about me
for the things that merit praise;
I will search for hidden beauties
that elude the grumbler's gaze.
I will try to find contentment
in the paths that I must tread;
I will cease to have resentment
when another moves ahead.
I will not be swayed by envy
when my rival's strength is shown;
I will not deny his merit,
but I'll try to prove my own;
I will try to see the beauty
spread before me, rain or shine;
I will cease to preach your duty
and be more concerned with mine.

— S. E. Kiser

 expect to pass
this way but once;
any good therefore
that I can do,
or any kindness that I can show to
any fellow creature, let me do it now.
Let me not defer or neglect it,
for I shall not pass this way again.

—Etienne De Grellet

foot and light-hearted
      I take to the open road;
   Healthy and free,
      the world before me,
The long brown path before me leading wherever
   I choose.
Henceforth I ask not good fortune, I myself am
   good fortune;
Henceforth I whimper no more, postpone no more,
   need nothing,
Done with indoor complaints, libraries, querulous
   criticisms,
Strong and content I travel the open road.
All seems beautiful to me.
I can repeat over to men and women:
You have done such good to me I would do the same
   to you.
I will recruit for myself and you as I go.
I will scatter myself among men and women as I go,
I will toss a new gladness and roughness
      among them.

— Walt Whitman

 ive for yourself —
live for life
Then you are
most truly
the friend of man

— Kahlil Gibran

 o not follow
where the
path may lead.
Go, instead, where
there is no path
and leave a trail.

— Anonymous

he best creed
we can have
is charity towards
the creeds of others.

— Josh Billings

od, give us grace
to accept
with serenity
the things
that cannot be changed,
courage to change the things
which should be changed,
and the wisdom to distinguish
the one from the other.

— Reinhold Neibuhr

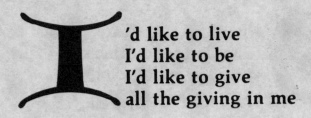

'd like to live
I'd like to be
I'd like to give
all the giving in me

— Hoyt Axton

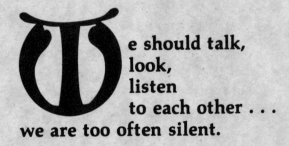

e should talk,
look,
listen
to each other . . .
we are too often silent.

— Judy Collins

We need to feel more
to understand others.
We need to love more
to be loved back.
We need to cry more
to cleanse ourselves.
We need to laugh more
to enjoy ourselves.
We need to see more
other than our own little fantasies.
We need to hear more
and listen to the needs of others.
We need to give more
and take less.
We need to share more
and own less.
We need to look more
and realize that we are not so
different from one another.
We need to create a world where
all can peacefully live
the life they choose.

— Susan Polis Schutz

WHAT I LIVE FOR

live for those who
   love me, for those who
   know me true;
For the heaven that
smiles above me, and awaits my spirit too;
For the cause that lacks assistance, for the
   wrong that needs resistance,
For the future in the distance, and the good
   that I can do.

— George Linnaeus Banks

his is my creed:
   To do some good,
To bear my ills
   without complaining,
To press on as a brave man should
   For honors that are worth the gaining;
To seek no profits where I may,
   By winning them, bring grief to others;
To do some service day by day
   In helping on my toiling brothers.
This is my creed: To close my eyes
   To little faults of those around me;
To strive to be when each day dies
   Some better than the morning found me;
To ask for no unearned applause,
   To cross no river until I reach it;
To see the merit of the cause
   Before I follow those who preach it . . .
To keep my standards always high,
   To find my task and always do it:
This is my creed — I wish that I
   Could learn to shape my action to it.

— S. E. Kiser

o more
than exist, live.
Do more
than touch, feel.
Do more than look, observe.
Do more than read, absorb.
Do more than hear, listen.
Do more than listen, understand.

— John H. Rhoades

ome on, let's live! It is so easy to die; so easy to give up; so easy to listen for the last note of Gabriel's trumpet. Come on, let's live! It is so easy to become discouraged; so easy to forget to wind life's clock; so easy to forget to shut the door on trouble; so easy to fail.
Come on, let's live! Let's be brave, and face today. It is our day. Let's meet trouble and conquer it. Let's use smiles to chase away the frowns.
Come on, let's live! Let's fill our hearts with the truth of purpose. Let's have hope for the future. Let's be honest and straightforward.
Come on, let's live! Let's look up and not down. Let's face the storms of doubt with determination to win. Let's have faith in God and self. Let's pray.
Come on, let's live!

— Everett Wentworth Hill

o be honest;
to be kind;
to earn a little
and to spend a little less;
to make, upon the whole,
a family happier for his presence;
to renounce, when that shall be necessary,
and not be embittered;
to keep a few friends,
but these without capitulation;
above all, on the same condition,
to keep friends with himself:
here is a task for all that a man has of
fortitude and delicacy.

— Robert Louis Stevenson

o live content with
small means; to seek
elegance rather than
luxury, and refinement
rather than fashion;
to be worthy, not respectable, and wealthy,
not rich; to study hard, think quietly,
talk gently, act frankly; to listen to
stars and birds, to babes and sages,
with open heart; to bear all cheerfully,
do all bravely, await occasions,
hurry never. In a word, to let
the spiritual, unbidden and unconscious
grow up through the common.
This is to be my symphony.

— William Ellery Channing

ive the best you have
received from the past
to the best that you may
come to know in the future.
Accept life daily not as a cup to be drained
but as a chalice to be filled with
whatsoever things are honest, pure,
lovely, and of good report.
Making a living is best undertaken as a
part of the more important business
of making a life.
Every now and again take a good look at
something not made with hands —
a mountain, a star, the turn of a stream.
There will come to you wisdom and
patience and solace and, above all,
the assurance that you are not
alone in the world.

— Sidney Lovett

THE WAY TO A HAPPY NEW YEAR

 o leave the old
with a burst of song;
To recall the right
and forgive the wrong;
To forget the things that bind you fast
To the vain regrets of the year that's past;
To have the strength to let go your hold
Of the not worth while of the days grown old;
To dare go forth with a purpose true,
To the unknown task of the year that's new;
To help your brother along the road,
To do his work and lift his load;
To add your gift to the world's good cheer,
Is to have and to give a Happy New Year.

— Anonymous

he best thing
is to give:
to your enemy,
forgiveness;
to an opponent, tolerance;
to a friend, your heart;
to your child, a good example;
to your father, deference;
to your mother, conduct that
will make her proud of you;
to yourself, respect;
to all men, charity.

— Francis Balfour

o awake each morning
with a smile brightening my face;
to greet the day with reverence
for the opportunities it contains;
to approach my work with a clean mind;
to hold ever before me,
even in the doing of little things,
the ultimate purpose toward which I am working;
to meet men and women with laughter
on my lips and love in my heart;
to be gentle, kind, and courteous through all
the hours;
to approach the night with weariness
that ever woos sleep and the joy that comes
from work well done —
this is how I desire to waste wisely my days.

— Thomas Dreier

PRAYER FOR EVERY DAY

Make me too brave
to lie or be unkind.
Make me too understanding,
too, to mind
The little hurts companions give, and friends,
The careless hurts that no one quite intends.
Make me too thoughtful to hurt others so.
Help me to know
The inmost hearts of those for whom I care,
Their secret wishes, all the loads they bear,
That I may add my courage to their own.
May I make lonely folks feel less alone,
And happier ones a little happier yet.
May I forget
What ought to be forgotten; and recall,
Unfailing, all
That ought to be recalled, each kindly thing,
Forgetting what might sting.
To all upon my way,
Day after day,
Let me be joy, be hope! Let my life sing!

—Anonymous

Grant that I may
not so much seek
to be consoled
as to console;
to be understood as to understand;
to be loved as to love;
for it is in giving that we receive,
it is in pardoning that we are pardoned.

— St. Francis of Assisi

DECALOGUE

I. Never put off till tomorrow what you can do today.

II. Never trouble another for what you can do yourself.

III. Never spend your money before you have it.

IV. Never buy what you do not want, because it is cheap; it will be dear to you.

V. Pride costs us more than hunger, thirst, and cold.

VI. We never repent of having eaten too little.

VII. Nothing is troublesome that we do willingly.

VIII. How much pain have cost us the evils which have never happened.

IX. Take things always by their smooth handle.

X. When angry, count ten, before you speak; if very angry, a hundred.

—Thomas Jefferson

ABRAHAM LINCOLN'S CREED

 believe in God,
the Almighty Ruler
of nations, our great and
good and merciful Maker,
our Father in heaven, who notes the
fall of a sparrow and numbers the
hairs on our heads. I recognize the
sublime truth announced in the Holy
Scriptures and proved by all history
that those nations are blessed whose
God is the Lord. I believe that the
will of God prevails. Without him,
all human reliance is vain. With that
assistance I cannot fail. I have a solemn
vow registered in heaven to finish the
work I am in, in full view of my
responsibility to my God, with malice
toward none; with charity for all;
with firmness in the right, as God
gives me to see the right.

 am not bound to win,
but I am bound to be true.
I am not bound to succeed,
but I am bound to live up
to the light I have.
I must stand with anybody that stands right,
stand with him while he is right,
and part with him when he goes wrong.

— Abraham Lincoln

n whatever arena of life
one may meet the challenge
of courage, whatever may
be the sacrifices he faces if he
follows his conscience —
the loss of his friends, his fortune, his
contentment, even the esteem of his fellow
men — each man must decide for himself
the course he will follow. The stories of past
courage can define that ingredient — they can
teach, they can offer hope, they can provide
inspiration. But they cannot supply courage itself.
For this each man must look into his own soul.

— John F. Kennedy

ord
make me
an instrument
of your peace.
Where there is hatred,
let me sow love;
where there is injury, pardon;
where there is doubt, faith;
where there is despair, hope;
where there is darkness, light;
and where there is sadness,
joy.

— St. Francis of Assisi

A DAY WORTH WHILE

I count that day
 as wisely spent
In which I
 do some good
For someone who is far away
 Or shares my neighborhood.
A day devoted to the deed
 That lends a helping hand
And demonstrates a willingness
 To care and understand.
I long to be of usefulness
 In little ways and large
Without a selfish motive
 And without the slightest charge.
Because in my philosophy
 There never is a doubt
That all of us here on earth
 Must help each other out.
I feel that day is fruitful
 And the time is worth the while
When I promote the happiness
 Of one enduring smile.

— Anonymous

rust to virtue and probity rather than to oaths. Counsel your friend in private, but never reprove him in public. Do not consider the present pleasure, but the ultimate good. Do not select friends hastily; but when once chosen, be slow to reject. Believe yourself fit to command when you have learned to obey. Honors worthily gained far exceed those which are accidental.

— Solon

t is in loving —
    not in being loved —
The heart is blest;
    It is in giving —
  not in seeking gifts —
We find our quest.
If thou art hungry, lacking heavenly food,
  Give hope and cheer.
If thou art sad and wouldst be comforted,
  Stay sorrow's tear.
Whatever be thy longing and thy need,
  That do thou give;
So shall thy soul be fed, and thou, indeed,
  Shall truly live.

                  — Anonymous

believe that the trials
which beset me today
are but the fiery tests
by which my character
is strengthened, ennobled,
and made worthy to enjoy the higher
things of life, which I believe are in store
for me. I believe that my soul is too grand
to be crushed by defeat; I will rise above it.
I believe that I am the architect of my own
fate; therefore, I will be master of circumstances and surroundings, not their slave.
I will not yield to discouragement;
I will trample them under foot and
make them serve as stepping stones
to success; I will conquer my obstacles
and turn them into opportunities.
I will not waste my mental energies

by useless worry. I will learn to
dominate my restless thoughts and look
on the bright side of things.
My failure of today will help to guide
me to victory on the morrow.
The morrow will bring new strength,
new hopes, new opportunities, and new
beginnings. I will be ready to meet it
with a brave heart, a calm mind,
and an undaunted spirit.
In all things I will do my best, and
leave the rest to the Infinite.

— Anonymous

ook to this day
for it is life
the very life of life
In its brief course lie all
the realities and truths of existence
the joy of growth
the splendor of action
the glory of power
For yesterday is but a memory
And tomorrow is only a vision
But today well lived
makes every yesterday a memory
of happiness
and every tomorrow a vision of hope
Look well, therefore, to this day!

— ancient Sanskrit poem

o keep young, every
day read a poem, hear
a choice piece of music,
view a fine painting,
and if possible, do a good action.
Man's highest merit always is,
as much as possible,
to rule external circumstances
and as little as possible
to let himself be ruled by them.

— Johann Wolfgang von Goethe

DESIDERATA

GO PLACIDLY AMID THE NOISE AND THE HASTE, AND REMEMBER WHAT PEACE THERE MAY BE IN SILENCE. ✺ AS FAR AS POSSIBLE, without surrender, be on good terms with all persons. Speak your truth quietly and clearly; and listen to others, even to the dull and ignorant; they too have their story. ✺ Avoid loud and aggressive persons; they are vexatious to the spirit. ✺ If you compare yourself with others, you may become vain or bitter, for always there will be greater and lesser persons than yourself. ✺ Enjoy your achievements as well as your plans. Keep interested in your own career, however humble; it is a real possession in the changing fortunes of time. ✺ Exercise caution in your business affairs, for the world is full of trickery. But let this not blind you to what virtue there is; many persons strive for high ideals, and everywhere life is full of heroism. ✺ Be yourself. Especially do not feign affection.

Neither be cynical about love; for in the face of all aridity and disenchantment, it is as perennial as the grass. Take kindly the counsel of the years, gracefully surrendering the things of youth. Nurture strength of spirit to shield you in sudden misfortune. But do not distress yourself with dark imaginings. Many fears are born of fatigue and loneliness. Beyond a wholesome discipline, be gentle with yourself. You are a child of the universe no less than the trees and the stars; you have a right to be here. And whether or not it is clear to you, no doubt the universe is unfolding as it should. Therefore be at peace with God, whatever you conceive Him to be. And whatever your labors and aspirations, in the noisy confusion of life, keep peace in your soul. With all its sham, drudgery and broken dreams, it is still a beautiful world. Be cheerful. Strive to be happy.

— Max Ehrmann

hink of the things
that make you happy,
Not the things
that make you sad;
Think of the fine and true in mankind,
Not its sordid side and bad;
Think of the blessings that surround you,
Not the ones that are denied;
Think of the virtues of your friendships,
Not the weak and faulty side;
Think of the hopes that lie before you,
Not the waste that lies behind;
Think of the treasures you have gathered,
Not the ones you've failed to find;
Think of the service you may render,
Not of serving self alone;
Think of the happiness of others,
And in this you'll find your own!

— Robert E. Farley

 o all the
good you can,
By all the
means you can,
In all the ways you can,
In all the places you can,
To all the people you can,
As long as ever you can.

— John Wesley

MY CREED

do not choose to be
a common man. It is
my right to be uncommon —
if I can. I seek opportunity —
not security. I do not wish
to be a kept citizen, humbled and dulled
by having the state look after me. I want
to take the calculated risk; to dream
and to build, to fail and to succeed.
I refuse to barter incentive for a dole.
I prefer the challenges of life to the
guaranteed existence; the thrill of
fulfillment to the stale calm of utopia.
I will not trade freedom for beneficence
nor my dignity for a handout. I will
never cower before any master nor bend

to any threat. It is my heritage to stand erect, proud and unafraid; to think and act for myself, enjoy the benefit of my creations and to face the world boldly and say: This I have done.

— Dean Alfange

y creed: — To love justice,
to long for the right,
to love mercy,
to pity the suffering,
to assist the weak, to forget wrongs and
remember benefits, to love the truth,
to be sincere, to utter honest words,
to love liberty, to wage relentless
war against slavery in all its forms,
to love wife and child and friend,
to make a happy home, to love the
beautiful in art, in nature, to cultivate
the mind, to be familiar with the
mighty thoughts that genius has expressed,
the noble deeds of all the world;
to cultivate courage and cheerfulness,
to make others happy, to fill life with

the splendor of generous acts,
the warmth of loving words;
to discard error, to destroy prejudice,
to receive new truths with gladness,
to cultivate hope, to see the calm
beyond the storm, the dawn beyond the night,
to do the best that can be done and
then be resigned. This is the religion of
reason, the creed of science. This satisfies
the brain and heart.

— Robert G. Ingersoll

I will this day try to
live a simple, sincere
and serene life;
repelling promptly every
thought of discontent, anxiety,
discouragement, impurity and self-seeking;
cultivating cheerfulness, magnanimity,
charity and the habit of holy silence;
exercising economy in expenditure,
carefulness in conversation, diligence in
appointed service, fidelity to every trust.

— John H. Vincent

MY CREED

o live as
gently as I can;
To be, no matter
where, a man;
To take what comes of good or ill
And cling to faith and honor still;
To do my best, and let that stand
The record of my brain and hand;
And then, should failure come to me,
Still work and hope for victory.

To have no secret place wherein
I stoop unseen to shame or sin;
To be the same when I'm alone
As when my every deed is known;
To live undaunted, unafraid
Of any step that I have made;
To be without pretense or sham
Exactly what men think I am.

To leave some simple mark behind
To keep my having lived in mind;
If enmity to aught I show,
To be an honest, generous foe,
To play my little part, nor whine
That greater honors are not mine.
This, I believe, is all I need
For my philosophy and creed.

— Edgar A. Guest

Write it on your heart that every day is the best day in the year. No man has learned anything rightly until he knows that every day is doomsday. Today is a king in disguise. Today always looks mean to the thoughtless, in the face of a uniform experience that all good and great and happy actions are made up precisely of these blank todays. Let us not be so deceived; let us unmask the king as he passes! He only is rich who owns the day, and no one owns the day who allows it to be invaded with worry, fret and anxiety. Finish every day and be done with it. You have done what

you could. Some blunders and absurdities
no doubt crept in; forget them as soon
as you can. Tomorrow is a new day;
begin it well and serenely and with too
high a spirit to be cumbered with your
old nonsense. This day is all that is
good and fair. It is too dear, with its
hopes and invitations, to waste a
moment on the yesterdays.

— Ralph Waldo Emerson

f we love love,
if we love friendliness,
if we love helpfulness,
if we love beauty,
if we love health,
if we love to create joy, if we love
usefulness and are not self-seekers,
the spirit which expresses itself in
love and helpfulness and beauty
will enter into us and abide there.
We become what we love.

— Anonymous

ake time to work —
it is the price of success.
Take time to think —
it is the source of power.
Take time to play —
it is the secret of perpetual youth.
Take time to read —
it is the foundation of wisdom.
Take time to be friendly —
it is the road to happiness.
Take time to dream —
it is hitching your wagon to a star.
Take time to love and be loved —
it is the privilege of the Gods.
Take time to look around —
the day is too short to be selfish.
Take time to laugh —
it is the music of the soul.

— an old Irish prayer

here are nine requisites
for contented living:
Health enough to make
work a pleasure.
Wealth enough
to support your needs.
Strength to battle with
difficulties and overcome them.
Grace enough to confess
your sins and forsake them.
Patience enough to toil
until some good is accomplished.
Charity enough to see
some good in your neighbor.
Love enough to move you
to be useful and helpful to others.
Faith enough to make real
the things of God.
Hope enough to remove all
anxious fears concerning the future.

— Johann Wolfgang von Goethe

Go forth with thy message
among the fellow creatures.
Teach them that they must
be guided by that inner light
which dwells with the pure heart, to whom
it was promised of old that they should
see God. Teach that each generation
begins the world afresh with perfect freedom;
that the present is not the prisoner of the past,
but that today holds in captivity all yesterdays,
to compare, to judge, to accept, to
reject their teachings, as these are shown
by its own morning sun.

— Ralph Waldo Emerson

If I had my
life to live over,
I would relax more.
I wouldn't take
so many things so seriously.
I would take more chances.
I would climb more mountains,
and swim more rivers . . .
Next time
I'd start barefooted
earlier in the spring
and stay that way
later in the fall.
I wouldn't make such good grades
unless I enjoyed working for them.
I'd go to more dances.
I'd ride on more merry-go-rounds.
I'd pick more daisies.

— Frank Dickey

Having achieved ninety-three
birthdays in this early life,
I wish to say that the
older we grow the more we
realize that life is worth the living.
We think too little of the fun there is in it;
we are too parsimonious of laughter.
The secret of happiness and longevity,
in my judgment, is to cherish and cultivate
cheerful, hopeful, buoyant spirits.
If you haven't them, create them!
Let us never lose our faith in human
nature, no matter how often we may be deceived.
Do not let such deceptions destroy confidence
in the real honest goodness, generosity,
humanity and friendship that exist in the world.
Believe me, they are overwhelmingly in the majority.

— Chauncey M. Depew

lways
remember
to forget
the things
that made you sad,
But never forget
to remember
the things
that made you glad.

— Elbert Hubbard

ay the road
    rise up to
  meet you,
    May the wind
be always at your back,
May the sun shine warm
  upon your face,
And the rain fall soft
  upon your fields,
And until we meet again,
May God hold you
  in the palm of His hand.

— an old Irish verse

ACKNOWLEDGMENTS

We gratefully acknowledge the permission granted by the following authors, song-writers, publishers and authors' representatives to reprint poems and excerpts from their publications.

Hoyt Axton for "I'd like to live," by Hoyt Axton. From the song ALICE IN WON-DERLAND. Copyright © 1970 & 1972 Lady Jane Music. International Copyright Secured. All rights reserved. Used by permission.

Robert L. Bell for "Desiderata," by Max Ehrmann. Copyright © 1927 Max Ehrmann. All rights reserved. Copyright renewed 1954 by Bertha K. Ehrmann. Reprinted by permission Robert L. Bell, Melrose, Massachusetts 02176

Contemporary Books, Inc. for "My Creed," by Edgar A. Guest. From COLLECTED VERSE by Edgar A. Guest, Copyright © 1934. Used by permission.

Grosset & Dunlap, Inc. for "We should talk," by Judy Collins. Edited version from THE JUDY COLLINS SONGBOOK, Copyright © 1969 by Judy Collins. All rights reserved. Published by Grosset & Dunlap. Used by permission.

Alfred A. Knopf for "Live for yourself," by Kahlil Gibran. From BELOVED PROPHET edited by Virginia Hilu. Copyright © 1972 by Alfred A. Knopf, Inc. Reprinted by permission.

Susan Polis Schutz for "We need to feel more," by Susan Polis Schutz. Copyright © Continental Publications, 1972. All rights reserved. From the book I'M NOT THAT KIND OF GIRL, published by Blue Mountain Press. Used by permission.

A careful effort has been made to trace the ownership of poems used in this anthology in order to obtain permission to reprint copyrighted material and to give proper credit to the copyright owners.

If any error or omission has occurred, it is completely inadvertent, and we would like to make corrections in future editions provided that written notification is made to the publisher: BLUE MOUNTAIN PRESS, INC., P.O. Box 4549, Boulder, Colorado 80306